To Anna and Catherine
on Madeline's 75th
Birthday 2014

To Anna and Catherine
on Madeline's 75th
Birthday 2014

MADELINE AND THE BAD HAT

Books About Madeline

Madeline
Madeline and the Bad Hat
Madeline and the Gypsies
Madeline in London
Madeline's Christmas
Madeline's Rescue

MADELINE
AND THE BAD HAT

WRITTEN AND ILLUSTRATED BY
Ludwig Bemelmans

PUFFIN BOOKS

MADELINE AND THE BAD HAT

To

Mimi

PUFFIN BOOKS
Published by the Penguin Group
Penguin Putnam Books for Young Readers, 345 Hudson Street, New York, New York 10014, U.S.A.
Penguin Books Ltd, 27 Wrights Lane, London W8 5TZ, England
Penguin Books Australia Ltd, Ringwood, Victoria, Australia
Penguin Books Canada Ltd, 10 Alcorn Avenue, Toronto, Ontario, Canada M4V 3B2
Penguin Books (N.Z.) Ltd, 182-190 Wairau Road, Auckland 10, New Zealand

Penguin Books Ltd, Registered Offices: Harmondsworth, Middlesex, England

First published by The Viking Press, 1957
Limited autographed edition, 1956
First trade edition, 1957
Viking Seafarer edition, 1968
Reprinted 1970, 1972, 1973, 1975
Published in Puffin Books, 1977
Reissued by Puffin Books, a division of Penguin Putnam Books for Young Readers, 2000

13 15 17 19 20 18 16 14 12

THE LIBRARY OF CONGRESS HAS CATALOGED THE PREVIOUS PUFFIN EDITION AS FOLLOWS:
Bemelmans, Ludwig, 1898–1962. Madeline and the bad hat.
Summary: When the Spanish ambassador moves in next door, Madeline and
the rest of the twelve little girls discover that his son is not the best neighbor.
[1. Stories in rhyme] I. Title.
PZ8.B425Mac7 [E] 77-1976
ISBN 0-14-050206-8

This edition ISBN 978-0-14-056648-2

Printed in China

In an old house in Paris
That was covered with vines
Lived twelve little girls
In two straight lines.
They left the house at half-past-nine
In two straight lines, in rain or shine.
The smallest one was Madeline.

One day the Spanish Ambassador

Moved into the house next door.

Look, my darlings, what bliss, what joy!

His Excellency has a boy.

Madeline said, "It is evident that
This little boy is a Bad Hat!"

In the spring when birdies sing
Something suddenly went "zing!"

Causing pain and shocked surprise
During morning exercise.

On hot summer nights he ghosted;

In the autumn wind he boasted

That he flew the highest kite.

Year in, year out, he was polite.

He was sure and quick on ice,

And Miss Clavel said, "Isn't he nice!"

One day he climbed upon the wall
And cried, "Come, I invite you all!
Come over some time, and I'll let you see
My toys and my menagerie—
My frogs and birds and bugs and bats,
Squirrels, hedgehogs, and two cats.
The hunting in this neighborhood
Is exceptionally good."

But Madeline said, "Please don't molest us,
Your menagerie does not interest us."

He changed his clothes and said, "I bet
This invitation they'll accept."

Madeline answered, "A Torero
Is not at all our idea of a hero!"
The poor lad left; he was lonesome and blue;
He shut himself in—what else could he do?

But in a short while, the little elf
Was back again, and his old self.

Said Miss Clavel, "It seems to me
He needs an outlet for his energy.

"A chest of tools might be attractive
For a little boy that's very active.

"I knew it—listen to him play,
Hammering, sawing, and working away."

Oh, but that boy was really mean!

He built himself a GUILLOTINE!

He was unmoved by the last look
The frightened chickens gave the cook.

He ate them ROASTED, GRILLED, and FRITO!
¡Oh, what a horror was PEPITO!

One day, when out to take the air,

Madeline said, "Oh, look who's there!"

Pepito carried a bulging sack.

He was followed by an increasing pack

Of all the dogs in the neighborhood.

"That boy is simply misunderstood.

Look at him bringing those doggies food!"

He said, "Let's have a game of tag"—
And let a CAT out of the bag!

There were no trees, and so instead
The cat jumped on Pepito's head.

And now just listen to the poor
Boy crying, "AU SECOURS!"
Which you must cry, if by any chance
You're ever in need of help in France.

Miss Clavel ran fast and faster
To the scene of the disaster.

She came in time to save the Bad Hat,
And Madeline took care of the cat.
Good-by, Fido; so long, Rover.
Let's go home—the fun is over.

There was sorrowing and pain

In the Embassy of Spain.

The Ambassadress wept tears of joy,
As she thanked Miss Clavel for saving her boy.

"Nothing," said the Ambassador,
"Would cheer up poor Pepito more
Than a visit from next door.

"Only one visitor at a time,
Will you go in first, Miss Madeline?"

So Madeline went in on tiptoe,
And whispered, "Can you hear me, Pepito?
It serves you right, you horrid brat,
For what you did to that poor cat."

"I'll never hurt another cat,"
Pepito said. "I swear to that.
I've learned my lesson. Please believe
I'm turning over a new leaf."
"That's fine," she said. "I hope you do.
We all will keep our eyes on you!"

And lo and behold, the former Barbarian

Turned into a Vegetarian.

And the starling and turtle, the bunny and bat,

Went back to their native habitat.

His love of animals was such,

Even Miss Clavel said,

"It's too much!"

The little girls all cried "Boo-hoo!"

But Madeline said, "I know what to do."

And Madeline told Pepito that
He was no longer a BAD HAT.
She said, "You are our pride and joy,
You are the world's most wonderful boy!"

They went home and broke their bread
And brushed their teeth and went to bed,

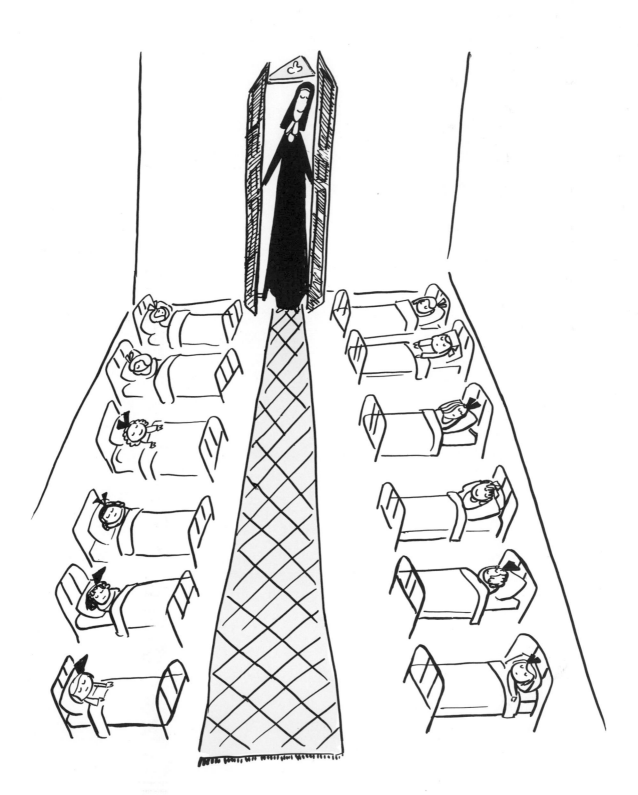

And as Miss Clavel turned out the light
She said, "I knew it would all come out right."